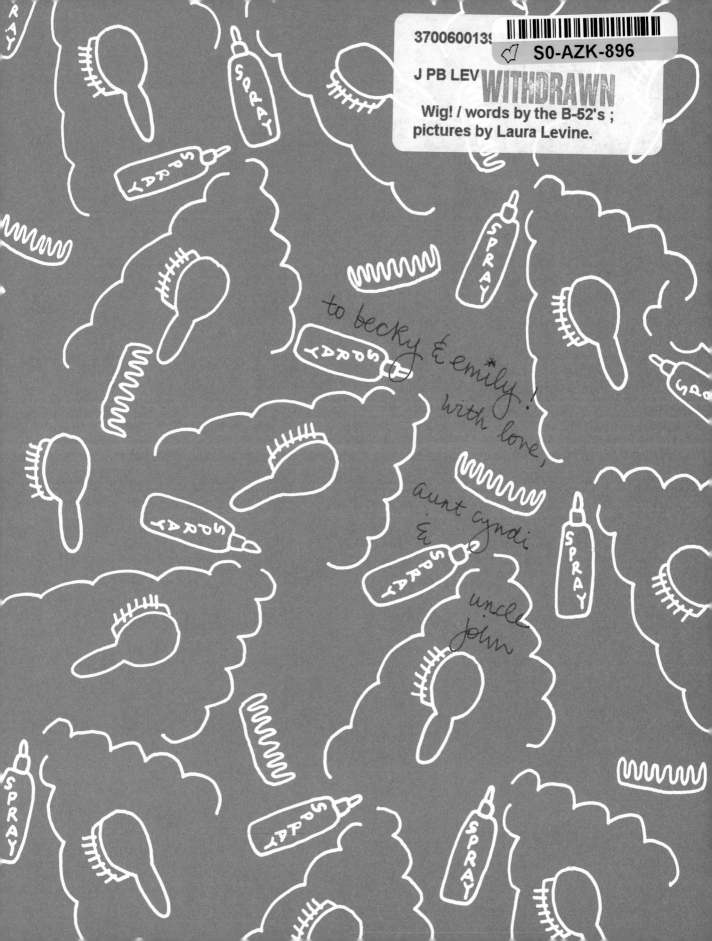

to becky & emily!
with love,

aunt cyndi
&
uncle
john

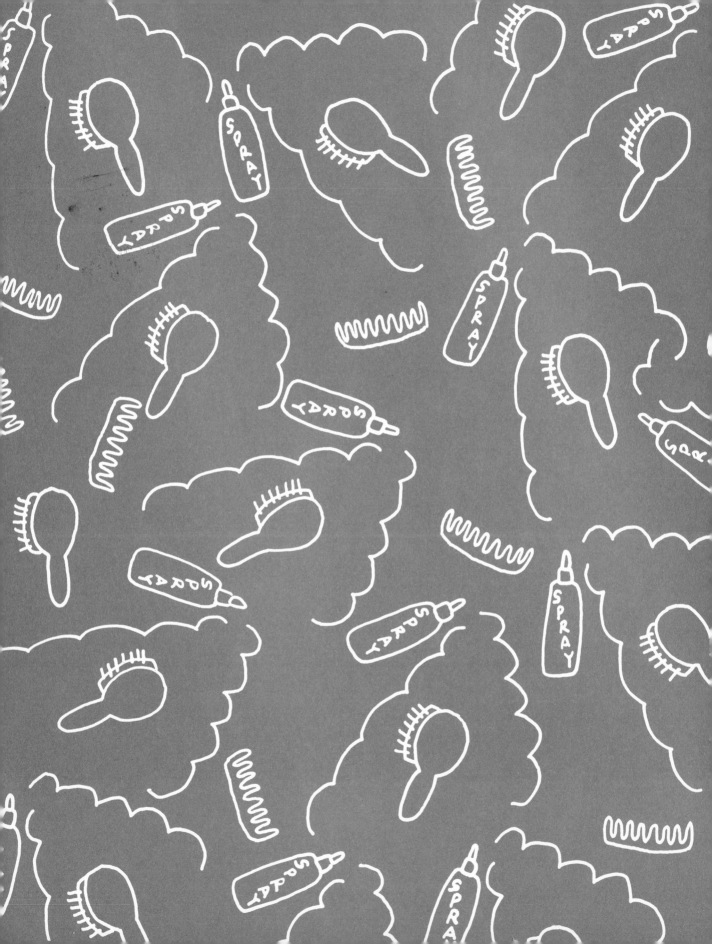

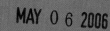

Wig!

WORDS BY *the B~52's*

PICTURES BY *Laura Levine*

Hyperion Books for Children / New York

Printed in Singapore.
For information address Hyperion Books for Children,
114 Fifth Avenue, New York, New York 10011.
FIRST EDITION
1 3 5 7 9 10 8 6 4 2

Library of Congress Cataloging-in-Publication Data
B-52's (Musical group)
Wig / by the B-52's ; illustrated by Laura Levine — 1st ed.
p.   cm.
Summary: Describes in pictures and words a variety of wigs and the
people who wear them. Based on a song by the B-52's.
ISBN 0-7868-0079-8 (trade) — ISBN 0-7868-2064-0 (lib. bdg.)
[1. Wigs — Fiction.   2. Hair — Fiction.]   I. Levine, Laura,
ill.   II Title.
PZ7.B1125Wi   1995
[E] — dc20   94-33486

The artwork for each picture is prepared using acrylic.

For Ricky Wilson
—K. P., F. S., K. S., C. W.

For Tommy
—L. L.

Sally's got a *wig.*

Ricky's got a **wig.**

Baby's got a *wig.*

Kate's got a *wig.*

I got

my wig

at the Diana Shop

with a purse to match.

Keith's got a **big** bouffant on.

We've all got *wigs* . . .

Julia's got a **wig**.

Phyllis has a *wig*.

Cindy's got a *wig*.

It's got a *wig*.

Carol's fall *fell*.

so let's go to the **neon** side of town.

START

THE
END

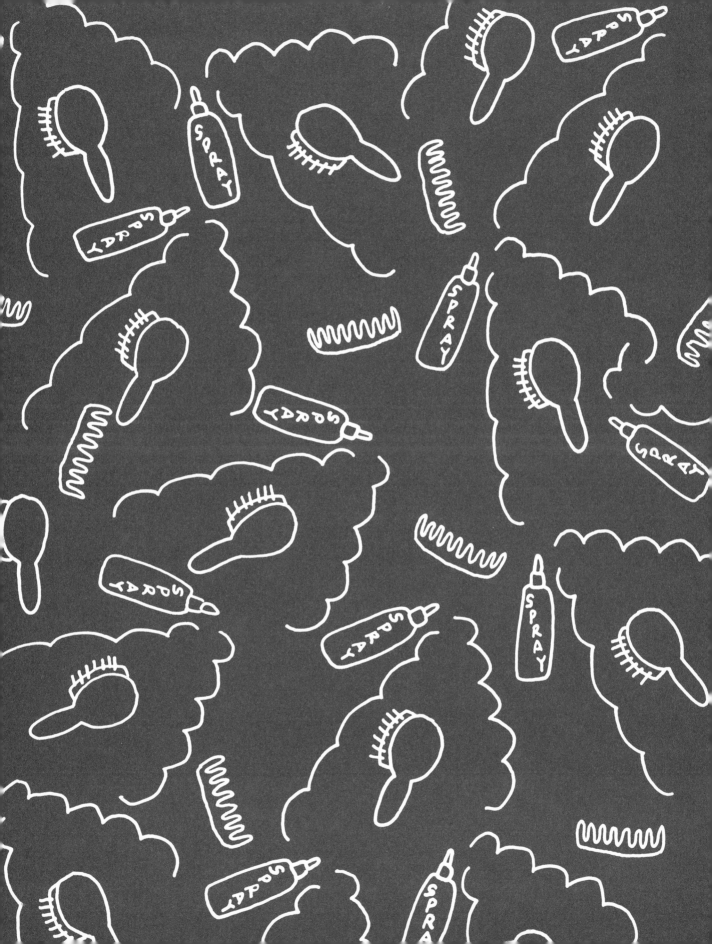

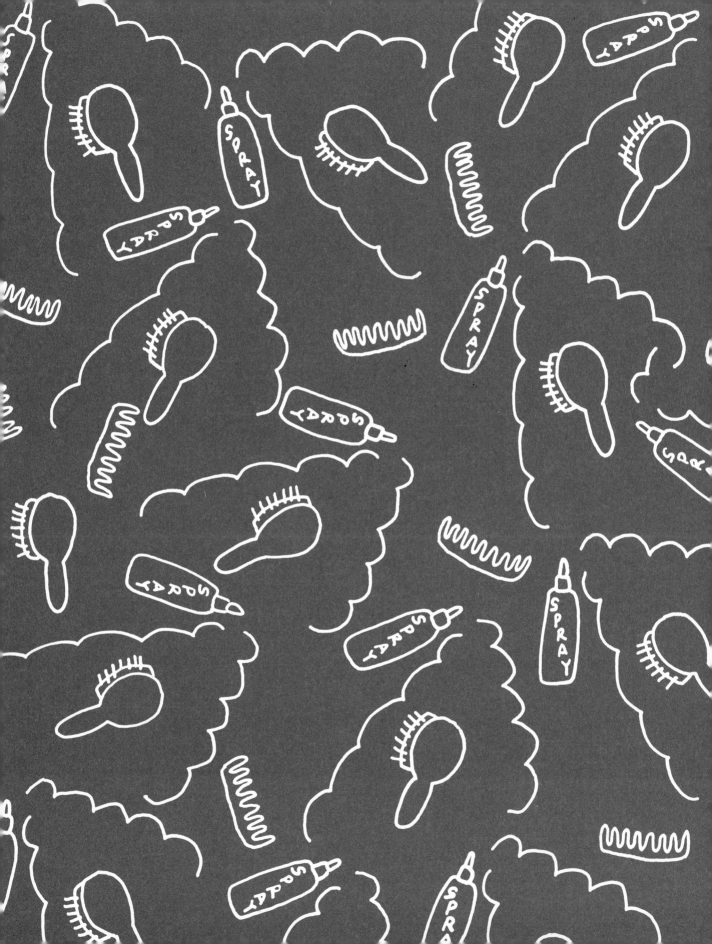